T0304569

Praise

"Brian Phillip Whalen has an incredible ear for dialogue, an eye for precise details, and a knack for delivering surprise after surprise, skills he deploys well through this excellent collection. The energy is relentless, each story a fresh burst of deep emotion and deeper wonder: once you start reading, you won't want to stop."

—Matt Bell, author of *Appleseed*

"There's the uncanny, then there are Brian Phillip Whalen's stories. In a realm of their own, his tales are populated by fragile human beings who can't believe their eyes and ears, yet through trial and error, march on. Whalen's writing is witty, surprising, frank, often tender, sometimes frightening. The striking voice and style in *Semiotic Love* emerge from a compelling mind, and a thoughtful reader of love shaped in the contemporary world."

—Lynne Tillman, two-time National Book Critics
Circle Award finalist, author of *Men and Apparitions*

"With the heart of Denis Johnson, the mind of a Zen master, and a deep, generous soul all his own, Brian Phillip Whalen has written a captivating, transcendent book. Whalen's shimmering sentences will make you laugh and cry and marvel and feel lucky to be alive. Smart money says you'll start rereading this extraordinary collection moments after you reach its final page."

—Edward Schwarzschild
author of *In Security* and *Responsible Men*

"Whalen is a master of the deadpan landing. His pith packs a punch. These fictions are our new wig and wag semaphores, transmitting, in bits and bytes, our encrypted and buried grammars of the heart. The [stories] that annotate and detonate *Semiotic Love* are like Hemingway's 'chapter' hint fictions that grout together the stories of *In Our Time*. They mine a muted telegraphy that scales up, in Whalen's hands, to the cumulonimbus diction and syntax of skywriting. I loved these mean little meanings."

—Michael Martone,
author of *Brooding* and *The Moon Over Wapakoneta*

"*Semiotic Love* bears the sign of a remarkable talent. Whalen is that rare writer who knows when to step aside and let his readers 'watch the sky fall apart.' With light and mercury, he exposes images of unprecedented potency—how better to speak of all our unspeakable loves?"

—JoAnna Novak,
author of *I Must Have You*

SEMIOTIC LOVE [STORIES]

SEMIOTIC LOVE [STORIES]

brian phillip whalen

Semiotic Love [Stories]
© 2020 Brian Phillip Whalen

First Edition, 2020

Published by Awst Press
P.O. Box 49163
Austin, TX 78765

awst-press.com
awst@awst-press.org

Printed in the United States of America
Distributed by Small Press Distribution

ISBN: 978-0-9971938-9-3
Library of Congress Control Number: 2020948583

Editing by Tatiana Ryckman
Copyediting by David McNamara
Book design and cover illustration by LK James

CONTENTS

III.

A story must be about what it is about
and continue to be about what it is about.

—Gordon Lish

I.

THE FATHER BELL

On his sixtieth birthday I gave my father a hammock, which he hung in a gazebo on a small hill overlooking the North Fork of the Shenandoah River. Lying there, suspended, he could pass the evenings staring at the unobstructed face of Powell Mountain, as the river *shushed* below.

Ten years earlier, my mother's diagnosis—pancreatic cancer—prompted their move to the country, my mother adamant that she not die *trapped in a web of suburbs.* Over the course of a year she yellowed and died, while my father waged war on the forest. Cord after cord of birch, red cedar, and oak, felled by hand and split and stacked in crooked rows scarring the yard. As the years passed, my father took to lecturing in public—to counter clerks, librarians, gas attendants—about the planet being *his*; he *lived* here; if he *wanted* a view, he'd *damn well* make one.

Nature kept encroaching. My father bought a chainsaw.

One balmy evening late in his life, I sat in the yard on a lawn chair reading Turgenev while up the slope my father, cradled in his sagging, weathered hammock, admired the first pink ribbons of dusk. The shallow river fled along its limestone bed; a lone hawk spiraled in the cloudless sky; a humid breeze, spongy with scents of wild sweet azalea and citrus-odored walnut husks, leaned through the trees. I could hear my father saying, "This feels good," repeating himself, again and again, until I hollered, "Be quiet!" The old man had rigged up a rope that when pulled caused the hammock to swing side to side: *this feels good, this feels good, this feels good.*

I still picture him, ten years dead, tugging that rope as if ringing a bell.

He was the bell.

[Sunday Brunch, Woodland Manor Nursing Home, Endwell, New York]

I like it better *here.*

Where do you think you are, Grandma?

Spokane, Washington!

MISSING

The child with one testicle inflates himself with God's blue air. Splay-legged, standing in the bed of a busted F-150, he belts "Welcome to the Jungle" over sunlit trees. Three yards away, the Malfets' beagles howl in their wire kennels, a dozen floppy dials tuned to Uno's frequency.

The gym kids started it. "A perfect name," said Celia, the woman Dad reminds him to call "*Mom,* dammit." Celia, running her fingers through his hair, telling him he's "*Uno* of a kind." She brought vinyl records and a turntable when she moved into their trailer. At night she'd school him in the history of rock and roll and in the morning hide messages inside his lunch pail. "Hold me closer!" "Love of my life!" "Sweet child o' mine!" Each weekday noon a yellow love song stuck to Fluff and jelly sandwiches. Uno's throat will tie off like a balloon if he so much as smells a tree nut. Case in point: Timmy Hillis slipped an almond in his pudding, and Uno's neck puffed up like a beaver's tail. His cries for help rose slowly, and thickly: an itchy growl closing off at the source. The sounds were dark, heavy, not sky-high like a siren or an angel or a song. Celia said the proof was in the pudding, "Dems da nuts." But Uno knew the *real* proof was his mother-mommy-*madre* suffered when she died. No bright and airy welcome to the Kingdom like the pastor promised. Only pain, and fear—each an unbearable weight.

"Mothers burn, and so do Indians," the gym boys chanted as they pinned him to the floor, twisting his wrists and ankles with their hands. Celia, drawing cool baths filled with oats and chamomile, kneeling beside the tub caressing his pink flesh while singing "I'm on Fire." She took him with her to church on Sundays where she sang boldly with the choir while he waited in a pew. For years he did not sing, and never prayed—an apprentice to his own suffering. Then one Sunday mass the choir sang a hymn about a tree "laden with fruit and always green." Uno heard the lyrics, but imagined them wrongly, dreaming not of a tree *de vida* but its opposite, a tree of *muerte*-murder-*fuego*, a nut-bearing tree, ablaze, and around its trunk the front end of a smoking pickup truck, crumpled like a juice box, and inside the cab his mother, trapped, suffocating, her rib cage cradling the steering wheel, her lips peeled back in silent prayer.

Choking on this image, as if it were a knot, Uno, in the church full of song, fell to his knees. And the sounds that rose from his small mouth? Not even dogs could hear.

NO TENGO

I flew to Paris with my girlfriend. We stayed at a cheap hotel at the edge of the red light district. Our concierge warned us not to stand too close to doorways—a criminal might pull us inside. It was a strange thing to say but I paid attention. On our last night in the city we ate dinner at a café a few blocks from our hotel. The waitress was the owner, and the chef her husband. The walls were decked in reds and greens, the tables made of solid oak. I'd never eaten escargot. It was delicious. My girlfriend, who'd been to Paris many times, ordered us a bottle of white, then a bottle of red. When the bill came, I was a little unsteady, but it was the waitress who fumbled with the handheld credit card reader. It would not operate, she said, more or less, in broken English. Her husband emerged from the kitchen, his forearms decorated with miniature wheels of cut chive. He too fumbled with the machine. He shook it and checked the batteries. My girlfriend found the whole thing funny, her bare toes crawling up my leg underneath the table, her neck and chest flush. "Can you bill our room?" I asked, my pulse quickening. I pointed toward the door. The waitress clapped her hands, looking pleased. Addressing her husband in French, she disappeared into the kitchen. The chef retrieved my coat from the rack. The waitress came back with a bottle of Chianti, filling my girlfriend's glass. My girlfriend, laughing, flashed me her thigh beneath her skirt, raising her glass to toast me out the door. It was raining. I followed the chef, who wore no coat and spoke no English. The night was cold and dark and I could feel the warm wine inside me. The chef was heading in the wrong direction but I followed him. I walked cautiously in the street while he sought cover from the rain on sidewalks, under awnings. He eyed me queerly as the rain soaked my coat. I tried to explain about doorways, the concierge, murder. It was only when I uttered *puerto* on a whim that we discovered both he and I spoke Spanish. *Un pocito.* I told him, more or less, what the concierge said, and the chef wrapped his hands around his throat, letting his tongue roll out. I went ahead and joined him on the sidewalk. We awning-hopped for several blocks until we found an ATM. I typed my passcode incorrectly. My hands were wet, and the buttons slippery. My card slid out without any cash, and the chef, watching over my shoulder, frowned. He began to walk off. I forgot the word *accidente,* so I called out: "*Por favor, tengo dinero!*" Just then, a tall man in a dark coat emerged from the shadows. I typed my passcode correctly and a menu appeared on the screen. But the tall man in the dark coat was heading our way, moving quickly in the rain. I canceled my transaction, stepping from under the awning. The man was in line behind the chef, and I motioned for him to go before me. The chef gestured for us to head back, but I touched his arm, said softly: *un momento.* I didn't think he understood. I thought about wringing my neck, or lolling out my tongue. I felt embarrassed, and queasy. I waited with the chef in the rain while the tall man used the ATM. By then the rain had washed all the herbs off the chef's arms and my coat was drenched. I pulled its collar to my throat while the chef resumed conversation. How long, he asked, had my wife and I been married? In correcting him I tried to find the words to tell him that my girlfriend and I were in college, and that after graduation we planned to move to New York City, where we'd get jobs and earn money and be happy, and no matter what we'd have each other, always. He did not seem to understand, though he smiled every time I said *amor*. He asked me how old we were. I said twenty-one and he burst into laughter. The tall man in the dark coat, having finished his transaction, joined us in the street. He said something in French to the chef, and the chef, pointing to my chest, said something back. Both men burst into laughter. Speaking rapidly, as if they were old friends, the two men conversed with joy. I stood there watching as their mouths contorted into wild smiles in the dim, foggy streetlight. The rain did not let up. There were no red lights in this neighborhood. Everyone was a liar and fraud. I stepped to the ATM and slid my card in the slot. Behind me the men carried on, laughing and causing a stir. I selected English from the menu. When prompted, I input random numbers. When my card slid out I acted surprised. I slid it in again, punched another set of random numbers. I stood to the side so the chef could see my movements. My hands were cold and shaking. I repeated the routine a few more times. By then the laughter had stopped, and the tall man walked off. The chef, sopping wet, turned up his palms. "*No tengo*," I said, and put my card in my wallet. His wife could bill our damn room, to hell with paying him cash. We headed back the direction we'd come, and the chef, still smiling, asked me more questions. I pretended like I did not understand. I had this feeling. I couldn't shake the image of my girlfriend, drunk in his café, or cafés like it, in Paris or Manhattan, her skin flush, her eyes inviting. I thought ahead to later that night, in our room, the way she'd look at herself in the mirror while letting her hair down, how she'd pull me close as we fell into bed, and as I walked with the chef in the rain I knew in my heart that I'd take her—but that she wasn't mine.

[How "Popa" Got His Name]

In December, 1980, when signing Christmas cards, he mis-spelled "Poppa."

EXPOSURE

Her junior year of high school, my sister won a contest for best photograph.

The way the story goes, it was a Sunday morning in Moscow. She'd been hiding under the ledge of a third-story window, kneeling beside Gabriel Boden, another exchange student, while the two of them threw hunks of stale bread at the old women walking home from church. Bored, my sister followed one of the women to a neighborhood park, a quiet spot with tree-lined fields. The woman, ten yards ahead on the path, stopped dead in her tracks. Her back to my sister, she stared into space, standing perfectly still—a living statue. There was no discernible reason. She stood there a very long time.

My sister, who brought her camera everywhere, took a picture.

When she turned thirty, my parents got my sister a digital camera. We hadn't seen her in a while and she wasn't staying long. She was "between programs" again, which meant another relapse was just around the corner. But still my parents hoped the camera would inspire her, maybe to take a family photo, or shots of the river and mountains. Maybe even think about returning to college. But she only took one photograph: a blurry image composed of the dog's nose, the corner of the coffee table, a crooked expanse of hardwood floor. She'd been trying to adjust the zoom when her finger brushed against the shutter button. "Thanks anyway," she said, excusing herself to the guest room. My mother placed the camera on the mantle, where it remained, untouched.

Two centuries ago, when daguerreotypes were new, it took fifteen minutes to pose for a photograph. Our ancestors had faith in transformation, abiding, in stillness, the expense of time it took to translate flesh and blood onto a plate of silvered copper. When loved ones passed on, those left behind could look to these images: keepsakes of the dead, sources of light in the darkness. But tell me, how do we recover *living* ghosts? How dark must it be to see their fading light?

DEEP WATER

I grew up watching fishing shows but never cared for fishing. My father deplored TV, and he dragged me to the river to get a firsthand feeling for the rod and reel. I was twelve the summer I hauled a five-pound fish from the deep black belly of the Susquehanna. When I saw what appeared to be a thin, black stripe along a bowed, silver body, my indifference turned to joy. "A sea bass!" I cried, mistaking the fish on my line for one I'd seen on TV. My father, removing the lure, exposed the sucker mouth. "It's a junk fish," he said, bending toward the water. My heart pounded, and the carp swam free.

I wrote a story around the same time a friend of mine wrote his. Both our stories had onions in them. My friend's onion was for curing boils and for soup. My onion resided in the belly of a magical dog. When I told my friend about the onion in my story, he cried plagiarism. I said, "An onion can't be plagiarized." He disagreed. "The principal onion," he said, "is the onion in my story. The onion in your story is an outer peeling of my onion. Your onion is a forgery, a germ. The onion in my story is the *true* onion."

Three nights later I was in bed reading Dōgen's

"Regulations for the Auxiliary Cloud Hall," a thirteenth-century Buddhist text:

> *Do not enter the hall intoxicated with wine. If you do so by accident you should make formal repentance. Do not have wine brought into the hall. Do not enter the hall smelling of onions.*

I thought, "How common the fisheries of the mind." I made a note to enlighten my friend about his counterfeit onion.

DOG

The drive to Alabama took us thirteen hours. We started in snow, and ended in rain. We stopped near Athens at a Country Inn. I'd made our reservation for the wrong week. It was January, a gray forecast. They had vacancies.

The dog slept between us in the bed.

In the morning, we ate breakfast at an IHOP. It was walking distance from the hotel. We left the dog alone in the room for an hour. It felt wrong, but we were hungry.

"Come noon," I told Mary, "and he'll never see us again."

We finished our pancakes. I wrapped my sausages in a napkin. I tore off little pieces in the car and fed the dog by hand. The dog stared at my fingers while I drove, waiting.

The Rescue smelled of antiseptic. Karen, the owner, replenished shallow plastic basins in the doorways with a bleach solution. She told visitors to dip their soles on entrance, and to cleanse again on exit. Hers was the only no-kill shelter within a thousand miles that had space for what we were offering. We did as Karen asked.

There were forty-nine dogs in residence: twenty-four

housed in outside kennels, twenty-five cordoned off in separate rooms inside her home. Karen lived upstairs, reserving the first-floor rooms by temperament: old dogs, shy dogs, horny dogs, sick dogs.

"Violent dog," I said.

"*Toothy*," she said, blotting her knuckle with gauze. "He'll live alone."

I filled out paperwork, while Mary—who I'd later discover had already fallen out of love with me, was preparing to leave me, was calculating how long she'd have to wait after the dog was gone to end things without looking heartless—held the leash and waited. I signed my name in blue ink while Karen led the dog to a temporary kennel, removed its collar, secured the latch. The dog barked behind me but I didn't look back. I dipped my feet in antiseptic, stepped into the day's gray light. I hurried down the driveway to the car until my dog's howls were lost among the others, and as we pulled away, I knew I'd hear that sound, that babel of unwanted dogs, on the long trip home, on the static on the radio, in the bursts of rain pulsing against the windshield, in the blizzard winds beating through the cornfields.

I still hear it.

[Tim: Newborn Daughter]

Let me give you two examples of my fear of everything.

AIR

Having lost the electric inflater, I sat opposite my father on the hardwood floor of my apartment as we took turns blowing air into the rubber nipple. We took our time, slow and steady, until the mattress reached a point of inflation where air escaped each time we took a breath. To offset our losses, we blew harder, and faster, and pretty soon we were feeling light-headed.

"In 'Nam," said my father, hugging the mattress with his tree-trunk arms, "they dropped me from twelve thousand feet with nothing but a bed sheet."

He huffed and puffed, and slid me the mattress.

I said, "I hope they let you keep the sheet."

"Get a job," he said, "and maybe you can buy a spare set for when your old man visits."

The mattress was a game of Pong between us, a rubber lung receiving and releasing air. I tried not to think about my father's slobber as I blew into the nipple.

"Hey," he barked, looking dazed. "Are you getting dizzy?"

"I'm not the one old enough to be wearing clothes designed by Kareem Abdul-Jabbar."

"True style never fades," said my father, adjusting his

thigh-cut blue nylon shorts.

"Only sanity," I said.

My father passed me the mattress, wet with sweat. It was one hundred degrees outside, and my air conditioner was busted. My father mopped his brow with a white cotton armband.

"When I caught touchdowns in college," he said, "I did backflips in the end zone."

I bit the nipple with my teeth, but air slipped out. I was, in fact, a little dizzy.

"No, dad—that was Uncle Skip."

And it was Skip, his older brother, who fought in Vietnam. My father was, it's true, in the Airborne Division, but he jumped from helicopters, not planes, and never more than fifty feet. He was too young for the draft, and the war was over by the time he joined the army. Skip enlisted sophomore year, and no amount of backflips could land him back in Jersey. He died in Khe Sanh.

"I'm high as a kite!" my father cried.

Our laughter came in bursts, our lungs demanding air before we could release it. Crying, I let go of the mattress and it flew like a balloon around the room, and we waved our arms as if we could reach it.

MEN

Erik lives in Asheville with a homeopathic nurse and six chickens.

On weekends in Los Angeles, Tim worries Jolene will make him "get going" before he's finished with his morning coffee; when he sets his cereal bowl in the sink, she reminds him to "put a little soap on it."

Jordan walks the streets of London searching for the longest route between his short-term flat and the National Archives; he wants his research on architectural drawings to take as long as possible to finish (her name is Marie).

Jeremy no longer wears the jester hat to parties.

Chad, who once had dreams of making the US Soccer Team, has babies (and a beer gut).

Liam lost another job because of internet pornography.

Kirk left home after college, married a circus acrobat, enrolled in divinity school, and has dreams of one day starting a "church for misfits" back in Buffalo.

Jessy grew six ears of corn in his garden, and for the first time in his life he feels self-worth.

Ray overcame his fear of disease to volunteer in Kenya, but he hasn't overcome his fear of Minnesota winters, and plans to move to California in the New Year.

David stayed in Iowa to raise a family with Sara; he still thinks getting published will fulfill him (good thing he spends more time with his children than he does on his novel).

Michael orders for his girlfriends in restaurants.

Josh is a librarian.

Gabe works in a lab curing cancer.

In another life, Thomas is a Norwegian film director shouting orders through a plastic cone, his body rising in the steel bucket of a crane overlooking a verdant fjord, while behind him, over Tromsø, the midnight sun—dangling on a plumb line—skirts the Arctic's untouchable blue.

TYPICAL

I was working as a waiter in Buffalo the year I saw two pairs of ducks in the city. I saw the first pair on my way to work at 6 a.m. on Main Street, in Williamsville, the wealthy suburb east of I-290. The cooks at the Original Pancake House refused to believe I'd seen two ducks in January. "Why did two ducks cross the road?" they joked, or, "Look! A woolly mammoth in the parking lot!" I hated the job, but needed money. Winter in Buffalo proved cold, and dark, and it didn't take many arguments at home, or many mornings dodging predawn traffic on the 33 while the lights of planes rose overhead, before my thoughts became preoccupied with flight.

In April, when I'd put enough away to get me out of Buffalo, I broke up with my girlfriend. But I hadn't thought about the lease we'd signed, or the remaining months' rent she'd have to pay by herself. I agreed to stay with her until she found a roommate, or until I'd saved enough to give her, in advance, an equitable portion of future rent. She told me not to worry about utilities. Her generosity was typical—if disingenuous—and maybe what prevented us from loving one another was we were too afraid to be ourselves, too frightened to risk honest feelings. It didn't matter, the die had been cast, and for the next few months I avoided the heartache of our dead relationship by working doubles, getting drunk on cans of Schlitz, and seeing movies by myself at Walden Galleria Mall. My girlfriend coped with the situation by volunteering weeknights at St. Joseph's Hospital, babysitting her sister's kids on weekends, and redecorating every inch of what would soon be *her* apartment. We avoided crossing paths but twice a day—once in the bathroom before work, and again in the hallway at night, she on her way to the bedroom, I to the couch where I'd sit for hours staring out the window at the cars parked on the street.

The night I moved out we went to Aaron's Diner for a final goodbye. My truck was packed to the hilt, and she had to squeeze in between me and all the stuff I had balanced on the bench seat: boxes of books, a bag of loose CDs, cans of food, a tool box, two lamps, a pillow. If a single thing shifted, the entire stack would collapse. So we suffered through proximity for the first real time in months, our bodies pressed together like a re-pinned grenade.

When we reached the parking lot, I helped her out of the cab and walked behind her along the diner's shrub-lined sidewalk, watching her long, straight hair swing flatly against her back. She had the hair of a librarian—or a church organist—and I always promised I'd wash it for her, like in a movie, but we never got around to it. The spring night was cool and clear and stars shone overhead. I could smell her jasmine conditioner, fry oil from the kitchen vents, pollen in the air. As we neared the diner's entrance, I heard a rustling in the bushes.

"Look," I said, touching her shoulder.

We squatted, side by side, peering beneath the green foliage of a shrub. A pair of ducks stared back at us. One of them, the male I imagine, ruffled its feathers.

She asked me, "What are two ducks doing at a diner?"

I could have said something—a joke to lighten the mood, or a sentiment to soften our hearts momentarily, to leave a small but honest connection between us, a parting kindness to survive the ruins of our failed relationship. I could've said a lot of things. I just didn't.

[Est. 1929]

On Main Street, his father, pointing to a stone engraving, says, "Bad year to start a bank."

HINDSIGHT

Tim's new stepdad owned a Cadillac. His name was Bob. He looked like Corbin Bernsen. Bob had a daughter, Bonnie, and I loved her. Bonnie smelled like coconut, and wore bikinis at the beach. When she walked along the waves, strands of her curly blonde hair pinched off in the straps on her back, trembling like kite string in the saltwater air.

Bob drove me, Tim, and Bonnie—and Tim's mother—to Fenwick Island, where he'd rented a house for the week. Bob's son, Peter, showed up a day late, drank gin and tonics with the grown-ups, and one night took a dump on a lifeguard tower. He bragged about it over breakfast. Bob said, "Wild child!" and Tim laughed so hard he choked on his Apple Jacks.

Tim thought Peter was a rock star. Peter called me "Smear the Queer." Bonnie said I needed "cultural assistance" and demanded I listen to Tori Amos on the Cadillac's Bose speakers. I owned two cassette tapes: *Sports* by Huey Lewis, and Kenny Loggins's *The Best of Friends*. Peter dared me to huff smelling salts, but I was too afraid, and everyone laughed. In the middle of the week I lost my glasses in the ocean, and Tim called me a douche.

"Now, now," Tim's mother said, and back at the house she laid her douche kit on the kitchen table. "*This* is douche," she said, and explained the procedure in scrupulous detail.

On our final night in Delaware, Tim, who loved Bonnie too, snuck into her room and stole the stuffed gorilla Bob had won her in a claw machine at the go-kart park. Tim punted the gorilla into the ocean.

"A sacrifice," he said, "for the damn gods of love."

I squinted into the wavering darkness, while the sounds from the nearby boardwalk married with the noise of the surf.

"Maybe the gorilla will find my glasses," I said.

Tim, shoving a clump of wet sand down my shorts, said, "*Douche*."

PALIMPSEST

My mother gave me a painting she'd made of a tree. "That," I told her, "is the ugliest thing I've ever seen." It was true—gray, meaty limbs resembled sewn-together parts of butchered horses; and oblong, crimson-colored fruit were disembodied organs. I refused the painting, referring to it as her "devil" tree. My mother, loathe to give in, adopted a new approach. She concealed the original image under a coat of red paint, and when the canvas dried, she painted a small black-and-yellow butterfly resting on a thistle. It was a simple, but effective, revision, and when I accepted the painting, my mother smiled. "When you were born," she said, "the doctor handed you over to me bottom-first, so I could see your genitals and know I'd had a boy. I was exhausted, and I didn't understand what I was looking at. I cried, 'What an ugly baby!'—and I held you."

II.

SEMIOTIC LOVE

[square one]

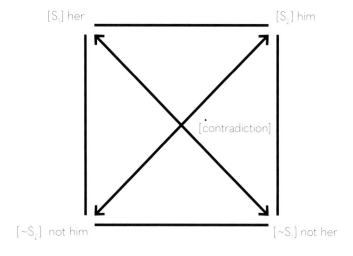

[S.] her   [S₂] him

[contradiction]

[~S₂] not him   [~S.] not her

We broke up. People saw it coming. How are things with you and Max? they'd ask. I'd lie, say, Same old, same old. I don't cover well; my eyes betray me. People nodded, knowingly. Best of luck, they'd say, or, Keep on truckin'. So it goes.

Him

I met her in line at T.J. Maxx. We were buying identical pairs of men's socks. In the parking lot, when I told her my name, she smiled. She waved the socks between us, gesturing at the marquee. This, she said, is a double coinkydink.

This is what she wrote with her finger on his back
while he slept:

The moon was pastried in the sky like a Nilla wafer.

Not Him

I ended it the day before our anniversary. I wanted Max and I to have something to look forward to, not back on. It made sense to me then. I was reading a lot of Emerson, transcendental flux, giant eyeballs floating in a wood. I preferred linearity, progression. Freedom of will not limited by precedent. A *real* new beginning, I told him. But Max, because he's Max, didn't care to dwell on such *significance*. He was more concerned with how we'd get out of our lease.

Things were great at first. I bought her a stuffed hippopotamus from the Jewel-Osco. She named it Wilbur and hugged it in her sleep until its snout was misshapen. We treated Wilbur like a son, played house, asked him at dinner how his day was at school. We cooked a lot, tried new recipes. Homemade bagels. Braised short ribs. Chicken fricassee from Alice B. Toklas's cookbook (that was her idea). She made the most awful pork dumplings, but I ate them. I told my friends, This is the girl I'm going to marry. I made wagers. I sized her finger while she slept. I'd tape notes to the bottom of her Nalgene bottle, copying quotes from the books on her shelves to show that I supported her work. I'd call her on the phone from the other room, just to say hello. I bought her cut flowers every weekend at the farmers market. Zinnias, her favorite. There was a time she'd even put them in vases.

[square two]

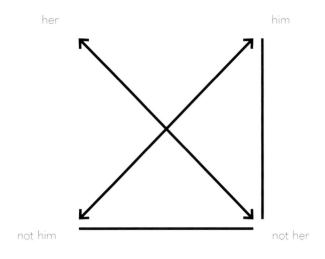

her   him

not him   not her

So what was wrong, exactly? People told me academics shouldn't date academics. It can get complicated, competitive. They said to look for love outside the university walls. A commoner provides stability, loyalty, simplicity. An average Joe. An ideal suitor. Enter Max. Max had an office job; a pet fish; a protestant work ethic. He was self-reliant, but not in Thoreau's sense of the word (Max wasn't about to build a shed). Max was Franklinesque, without knowing it, of course. *His* books were balanced (mine were strewn across the bedroom floor like dirty socks). So what was it, then? In a word—*sex*. In bed, I wanted minstrelsy, subversion, pomp. I wanted everything, and not just anything would do. My desires were kinky, complex. His were not. I wanted jouissance, replete, never-ending. He wanted, simply, *me*.

Him

I want gum, she said. I've got some Juicy Fruit, I said. Jujyfruits? she asked. The train was loud, filled with passengers. No, I said, *Juicy* Fruit. Oh, she said. She looked at her watch. I want *bubble* gum, she said, not chewing gum.

This is what her dreams were like:

a gender is a gender is a gender is an imitable diachronic set of acts reified as *a priori* biological fact is a gender is an imitable diachronic set of trait acts reified as *a priori* objects-in-themselves is a gender verb [asterisk] indefinite article sex-enactment indefinite article stylized repetitions *congealed-over-time* onto/epistemological paradox with a side of semantic au jus is [twenty-five-page term papers] a gender is a gender is a gender

Not Him

I almost forgot. At his company's Fourth of July picnic in Millennium Park, he kissed some slut named home-wrecker.

I said, Where's the beef? and she laughed so hard she snorted popcorn up her nose. We were watching the second *Matrix* movie on DVD. She blew the popcorn into a tissue and I said, Yuck.

[square three]

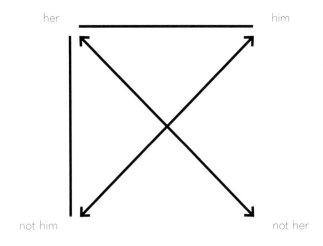

her   him

not him   not her

Mise-en-scène: the shower, a brush. I'm not wearing paint, he said. It's edible, I said. I'm a *man*, he said, not a canvas. I protested: How can I be Betsy Ross if you won't be the flag? That's bull, he said, just be yourself. I'm Queen Dido on a spire! I said. I'm Paris fucking Hilton on a binge! No, he said, you're you. I only want *you*. He reached out to hold me. I backed away. Me? I said. I'm *me*? Then who the hell are you supposed to be?

47

Him

I'd hold her socks in my hand, sometimes her shoes. Just to feel closer to her. One time she told me to hold a hair clip while she fixed her bangs, and I watched her eyes in the mirror, and knew.

Hung from brackets, Edmund H. perceived the ob-
jects of the world; the world, in turn, perceived [sigh];
Heidegger removed a Jew in 1941; now in some alleyway
in Freiberg a cat says moo and a pair of shadowy brackets
floats across the River [oh fuck me] Asterisk…

Not Him

What's this word? he said. First it was *vita.* Then *aleatoric, eschewed, anabasis.* It means, I said, to rub against strangers in public, for sexual gratification. He read my poem again, aloud this time: *…the celestial frottage of asteroids…* He stroked his chin, pretending to be lost in thought. I could have put a knife in his face.

We watched an improv show near Wrigley. When we got home, I said, I think I could do that. Drive a cab? she asked. No, I said, be funny, on stage. Oh, she said, pouring herself a glass of zinfandel. I grabbed an orange off the kitchen counter. You don't think I'm funny? I said. She sipped her wine, slowly, watching me peel the rind. Maybe you could take a class, she said.

[contradiction]

The Crux of Their Dilemma

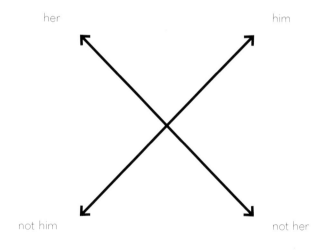

her   him

not him   not her

This doesn't, he said, shed light on anything. Read it aloud, she said. *The visual representation of the logical articulation of any semantic category or, in other words, the visual representation of the* CONSTITUTIVE MODEL *describing the elementary structure of signification.* That, she said, is a semiotic square. That, he said, is a ridiculous bit of nonsense. No, it isn't. Yeah, he said, it friggin' is. Keep reading! she said. *In the Greimassian model, given a unit of sense* S1 (e.g., rich), *it signifies in terms of relations with its contradictory* ~S1 (e.g., not rich), *its contrary S2 (e.g., poor), and the contrary of* S2~S2 *(e.g., not poor).* Exactly, she said, Clear as day. He closed the book, emphatically. Pure [nonsense], he said. [~S1], she said back. Well, he said, it certainly doesn't make any [S2]. It doesn't *not* make [S2], she said. Yes it does, he said, deliberately so. You're suggesting, then, she said, that Gerald Prince defines a semiotic square in such a way as to *purposefully* create [S2] out of [S1]? [~S2], he said, only [S1]! There's no [S2] in any of this! He jumped up to leave; she took a deep breath. You just don't get it! they cried out in unison. He took the book off the bed and threw it out their open window. It landed in the empty courtyard pool below.

[square four]

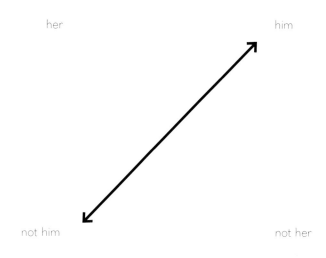

her   him

not him   not her

He shaved his beard for me, because it scraped my neck during sex. He came out of the bathroom with a stupid grin on his face. He looked like a pumpkin. I'm Jeremiah Johnson, he said proudly. Hmm, I said. He waited, fresh and alcoholic, for a better reaction. I suppose, I said, and I paused. I tried smiling, but it was too late. He shook his head. Of course! he said, and threw up his hands.

Him

I'm going to make a sound, I said. I want you to translate. She was lying flat on a stone wall, her head in my lap. Shoot, she said. I said, *Bwawk!* A noun, she said. A way in which to be perceived by sand. I said, *Floopswee*. Verb, she said. To cause to be dismayed. I stroked her temples, her eyelids, her nose. I think you ought to marry me, I said. Adjective, she said, to tend to press the issue. The sun was setting behind the city, the lake growing dark, the rocks beneath the surface disappearing one by one. *Grabble*, I said. That's a word, she said, and we left.

Read Goethe in a cherry tree. Read Bukowski in a bus terminal. Don't read Shakespeare. There's no place like the beach for Lawrence Durrell. Read Virgil in the candlelight. Read Henry James with a High Life; read Horkheimer with a donut; the Prison Bitch, birth thereof; oh Fartor Refartus; for fuck's sake leave me alone…

Not Him

I whispered in his ear: Rice-A-Roni, the San Francis-*coooo* treat! He just lay there, snoring like a toad. I said it again but nothing happened. I closed my eyes and started counting. One thousand one hundred and sixteen snores later, it was morning. The alarm rang. He yawned, nuzzling the side of my neck. Sleep well? he asked. Like a baby, I said.

We took the train in the wrong direction. We'll be on time, I said. But the train didn't stop at the next station. It ran express toward Evanston. On the platform at the Howard stop, she tapped her foot until I touched her leg. We stood beside each other, waiting. I said, We could *rent* a movie?

[square five]

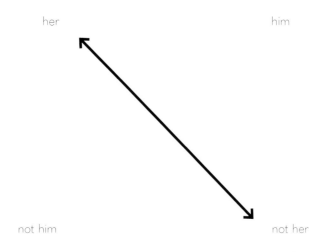

her

him

not him

not her

What do you love about me? I asked him. He didn't think long about it. Everything, he said. We were in the grocery store, buying coffee, ice cream, bread. I stepped into a main aisle. Even this? I asked. I turned my palms to the ceiling, raised the roof while making *woot-woot* noises. People noticed. He pretended not to care, tossed a bag of Seattle's Best into our cart, and walked away. I caught up with him at the deli counter. When I held his hand, he blushed. You're weird, I said. *Me?* he balked. He let go of my hand, acting angry. But he couldn't hide his smile.

Him

She was always doing something strange, especially in bed. From time to time I'd go along with it, but nothing ever seemed to make her happy. Even if she got her way, she'd cry. She'd stare at herself in the mirror. Her breasts, her hips, her ears. She'd press her thumbs into her cheekbones. I'd find her lying on the bathroom floor, sobbing, and she'd run the shower for hours, hot steam invading our bedroom through the crack under the bathroom door. I'd leave a glass of water for her on the nightstand, grab my keys, take a walk around the neighborhood. I always came back.

This is what he could never understand:

The swift, instructive nature of a theory bomb. *Parole*—his teeth; *la langue*—her legs. This is how her universe presents itself. Aporia, desire, career, oh God, oh God, oh God! [Alfred Jarry's zombie licks the phlegm napkined off the wiry ends of Slavoj Žižek's beard, while Karl Marx and Harry Potter duel over a girl, leaving each with a scar.] She *could* have loved him, yes, perhaps—if she'd never read Baudrillard, never had a father, never watched TV.

Not Him

I put a finger in his mashed potatoes, smoothing them with my fork before he saw the indentation. *Millionaire* was on TV. The question dealt with popular novels. Hey, he said, you should know this one. He forked his potatoes, took a bite. I watched him chew, fascinated by his ignorance. It used to be cute, his feigned interest in my work. I said, I'm a scholar of American literature, babe. But isn't John Grisham American? he said, eyes on the screen. I stuck another finger in his food.

Not Her

Don't cry, I said. I'm here, I said. But where in that head of hers was she?

[square six]

her   him

not him   not her

That's Cornel West, I said. Who? he asked, his hand in the popcorn bowl. I said, The black dude with the killer afro. No, he said, I mean who's Cornel West? I bit my lip. I watched his jaw moving up and down. Then I licked my finger, twisting it in his ear. He brushed me off. Stobbit, he mumbled. I rested my head on his arm. I felt happy that night. I felt safe.

We took a weekend trip to Madison. I liked the bike paths. She liked the libraries. We ate sushi twice a day. I made jokes about cheese. She listened to Joni Mitchell's *Blue* album on repeat the entire drive back. When we got home, we watched *ElimiDate*, and she patted my leg each time a guy got booted. After that night, nothing. She stopped. Stopped everything. Not a touch, not a kiss, not a smile. I tried to talk to her. She'd say things like, I'm a clock without hands, or, Don't put me in a drawer. She spent all her time writing a paper on *The Sound and the Fury*. She didn't eat. She slept on the couch. When I held her, she no longer bothered to push me away.

This is what she's afraid people understand about her that she doesn't understand about herself:

When pressed, she can't distinguish A from P; she brings up N or D or M and E, and says she "much prefers," hoping that ends it; she sees herself as someone else, the abject remainder of billboards and tubes; she celebrates loyalty, but never in public; her yoga coach is cute like Maggie Gyllenhaal; behind her pessimism is a secret faith in Dionne Warwick; sometimes she thinks about the shape and weight of boxing gloves, telephones, hats without brims; the sight of a skyscraper makes her nipples erect; being in the classroom makes her yearn for canopies, tents, fire drills; she's a sycophant to those with undeserved power; she seeks approval from everyone, while mocking normality; at night her toes get cold; every so often, her protests become prayers.

Not Him

When I met him, zap, I thought that was it. I'd tell people, Sometimes life has a way of dropping magic in your lap. Bleh. Magic has a way, also, of making *itself* disappear. *Poof.* Ta-fuckin'-da. Ex nihilo, and reverse. The rabbit, the hole. Tell me, was I ever surprised?

At a Fourth of July fireworks display in Millennium Park, I thought to myself, Why the hell not? and I kissed a coworker named Rachel. It was only the once, and it wasn't wonderful. But it was real, you know, she kissed *me*, and what else matters in the end?

BROADCAST

I'm reading the diaries of Marcus Aurelius beside my third-story window on a brisk, sunny autumn day in Albany, New York, when I hear a man singing on the sidewalk. I put my face to the window, as I do nights when college couples argue drunkenly in the street. The man is standing by a row of garbage cans. I've seen him before—he's homeless. Today, he holds a brown paper bag, and hosts a radio show. "Ladies and gentleman, Michelle Smith is a liar and a fraud. Now another hit from the 1950s." A dime-store cowboy, he sings an iterative, plaintive lament that suits his forlorn voice. His rusty baritone is one pack shy of a voice box. He belts out half the chorus, drinks from his paper bag, then delivers the end of the chorus. In lieu of a bridge, he repeats the line about that woman, Michelle Smith, liar and fraud. He loops again: a verse, half the chorus, a swig, the end of the chorus, Michelle. I don't recognize the song; I write its lyrics in the cover of my *Meditations*. Just then a bird lands on my oriel. It's a goldfinch, I think: a yellow belly, black wings. Fugitive harbinger. And the homeless man—an auger? Michelle Smith—a signal; a symbol; a *sister*? I watch the bird until the bird flies off. I lower my head and read about Rome.

My sister is a homeless opioid addict living in Richmond, Virginia. She will never leave her city, where she knows the location of all the shelters, churches, dealers, and the abandoned Section 8s. Some nights my sister sleeps under a bridge. Other nights she's a prostitute. She emails—off and on—when she gets hold of a GoPhone, or a man she spends the night with has a Wi-Fi connection. I send my replies, and weeks go by. Months. Two years once lapsed before I heard from her.

At noon, the man is still hosting his show. I've had enough meditations for one day. I put away the book of stoic aphorisms, and open my laptop. The first hit I get on the lyrics is the 1954 film *The Outcast*. "Yesterday's gone / love me from now on / be true to me / forget about the past." There's a Ricky Skaggs version. A Willie Nelson cover, too. And one by Billy Walker. The internet tells me the original was written in 1955 by Webb Pierce and Cindy Walker. Pierce was a honky-tonk musician. A reviewer on amazon.com argues that Pierce's songs are not "well-preserved" enough by artists, citing a discrepancy in the number of covers of Pierce's songs compared with covers of the other luminaries of the '50s and '60s. *Preservation. Cover. Protection.* Something tells me the search I'm running is a foxhole without a fox. The name "Michelle Smith" returns too many hits. The internet can't give me what I'm looking for. I listen to the song online—it sounds all wrong.

*

The homeless man moved on. But I'll remember his song gave weight—*the tragic?*—to a sunny morning in a city where I never felt at home. I don't know if I'll see him again, but I'll see others, men and women both, coming to the city seeking shelter, having just arrived, perhaps, by Amtrak, the way my sister might have if she ever had the urge to find me. And had she, she'd have stepped off the platform at the station in Rensselaer, across the Hudson, and looked, like others before her, to the west, over Dunn Memorial Bridge, to the city beckoning, like a token gleaming in the night, and she'd have learned what they do, that the city from far away looks clean, well-lit, and small: a museum display—an exhibition called "The Promise."

BROTHERS

I visited Prague with a friend who was vegan. Our final night in the city, we stopped at a vegan-friendly pub after attending a classical concert in a church by the Astronomical Clock. My friend, tired of eating salad and bread, read an online review of the pub, which was owned by two brothers. We hadn't eaten since breakfast, having walked a great distance that day, over the snow-covered rail lines to the cemetery where Kafka was buried, to the KGB Museum in Malé Strana over a long bridge spanning the cold Vltava River, then back to our hotel room to change for the concert.

In the church, the quartet played Vivaldi's *The Four Seasons*. The acoustics were lovely.

When we arrived at the pub, we were famished. Our first pints of pilsner went straight to our heads, and we found ourselves in good spirits, swapping old stories—collegiate foibles, long-lost crushes, adolescent gripes, and teenage rivalries—and sharing hopes for the future. My friend was getting married in May to a girl he'd been dating, off and on, since college. I was heading back to school in the fall to start a PhD program, so I could finally learn to grow up—and to teach. Our trip was a de facto two-man stag party, a send-off to bachelorhood and, by default, our youth. We spent the better part of the week eating and drinking and walking the city, taking in its sights, museums, and different brands of absinthe. We'd arrived the day after Christmas, and the city streets, though violently cold, teemed with festivity. The entire trip—save for the absinthe—felt like one never-ending snow day.

The barroom smelled of paprika and lager. Now and again a bell over the pub's door chimed and the younger of the two brothers strode briskly through the kitchen doorway, hopped around the bar, and met each guest with the same joviality with which he'd greeted my friend and me when we'd first arrived. He sat new parties in the adjacent dining room. My friend and I sat at the empty bar.

The younger brother poured drinks, and served as waiter. He was short and thin, while his brother was tall and fat, and the contrast between them entertained us. The older clean-shaven; the younger a mustache. The older balding; the younger a mop of shoulder-length hair. The younger a T-shirt and jeans; the older black slacks and a dress shirt, and a tie slung over one shoulder.

A metal cart in the doorway between the bar and kitchen acted as a preparation zone—a pass—where the older brother dropped off plates of food for the younger to garnish, then serve. The older brother never smiled, and we only ever saw him at the pass. We imagined years of pent-up ire, the older man slaving away over hot humid stoves, while his younger brother combed foam off cold pints and entertained guests. There must have been a good number of tables in the adjacent dining room, judging from the quantity of food coming out of the pass. Plates piled high with steaming dumplings and meats. Bowls brimming with goulash and gravies.

After a second round of pilsner, I ordered the braised brisket with dumplings. My friend, the vegan, ordered a house specialty: cabbage stew made with seitan, not sausage.

We were finishing our third pint of *pivo*, feeling warm in the belly, and light in the head, when the younger brother, looking contrite, entered the barroom. He brought with him the scents of baked mincemeat and garlic, but no food. My friend's stomach rumbled so loudly it rattled my barstool.

"I am sorry," said the brother, thick with accent. "My brother"—he gestured toward the kitchen—"he has a mistake. Okeydokey?"

He poured us another round of pilsner on the house. He poured one for himself and raised his glass. The three of us drank. Setting his elbows on the bar top, he asked where in America we were from. He asked how long we were staying in Prague, and if we saw the Smetana museum. He asked if we liked American music. We said yes, we did, and an uncharacteristic smugness washed over his face. He exuded a strange, wily confidence. Even his bar rag looked proud. In broken English he explained he was a "connoisseur" of American music, then he downed his pivo in a single gulp, walked the length of the bar to the pass, and reached, standing on his tippy toes, to a stereo on a shelf above the cart. The speakers—which had thus far been playing piano sonatas by Mozart—fell silent. He pushed a series of buttons on what we discovered was a multidisc player.

The song he'd chosen for us was "Funkytown" by Lipps, Inc.

The song's plucky synthetic bass notes progressed in rhythm until a cartoony kazoo-like keyboard blared its unmistakable lick. The younger brother raised the volume to an ear-piercing decibel. He gave us thumbs-up, a gleam in his eye. He then disappeared into the kitchen.

Moments later, the older brother appeared in the doorway, delivering food to the pass. He reached to the high shelf, which, given his height, took no great effort, and pressed a button on the stereo. "Funkytown" fell silent. Mozart was restored—an adagio, dulcet and calming. He adjusted the volume, and returned to the kitchen.

The younger brother appeared in the doorway, making subtle movements to garnish, we surmised, the plates his brother had dropped off. He looked at us over his shoulder, furtively. He put a finger to his lips and reached to the shelf. As "Funkytown" picked up steam he turned up the volume, rocking his head while carrying four delicious-smelling meals—two in one hand, one in the other, and a fourth skillfully balanced on his forearm—around the bar and into the dining room, giving us a wink on his way.

Moments later, the older brother appeared in the doorway. Mozart came back, the volume reduced. He did an about-face step into the kitchen.

Our pints were empty. When the younger brother returned to the barroom, he refilled them. On his way into the kitchen, he stopped in the doorway, reaching up to the shelf, and waltzed off.

Moments later, the older brother appeared in the doorway, reaching straight for the shelf.

When the younger brother returned to the bar, he smelled like cigarettes. Mozart had played for two, maybe three, sonatas. Without word about our meals, which had not arrived, he poured us free shots of a black digestive called Becherovka. He poured himself a shot, raised it up, said, "Na zdraví," then pounded the empty glass on the bar top. The bitters tasted of cinnamon and sugar-free cough drops, and he described, more or less, its infusion process, which involved the extraction of oils from dozens of herbs and spices, a full list of ingredients kept secret since the early 1800s.

On his way to the kitchen, he stopped in the doorway and reached for the shelf.

talk about it

talk about it

In his absence my friend and I discussed the wedding, brainstorming ways that I could navigate my best man speech without his wife, who rarely approved of my antics, tossing champagne in my face or spreading rumors to the available bridesmaids. But we couldn't concentrate: Lipps, Inc. was distraction enough, but the fracas in the kitchen was overwhelming—a heated argument, we presumed, between the two brothers.

Eventually, the older brother appeared at the pass. As *Moonlight Sonata* began, my friend and I stifled our laughter. My friend stared at his feet, clenching his teeth. I had to excuse myself to the restroom, hurrying down a narrow flight of stairs, nearly toppling over as I followed a cellar hallway that led back in the direction of the bar. The ceiling down there was so low I had to stoop to fit under the bathroom's doorframe. My friend, who was about as tall as the older brother, would have had to squat while taking a piss.

As I flipped up the lid, I heard, from above, the opening measures of "Funkytown."

The bathroom was painted white, with white tile floor, and no artwork adorned the walls, and occupying that space felt aseptic and dreamlike. The sensation I had was akin to the feeling one gets in a surgical waiting room, or an airport lounge, except for the lowness of the ceiling, the floorboards above me so close to my head I could feel the bass notes of "Funkytown" vibrate my teeth. I must have been near to, or under, the pass, and as my stream died out I heard a ruckus overhead, followed by the unmistakable sound of shattering glass. It occurred so near to my head, I ducked on instinct. Next came a thunderous noise, one that caused the toilet water to ripple.

The music fell silent. I flushed.

A fresh-drawn pint, gold and foamy, waited for me on the bar, perspiring into its coaster. My friend was in full hysterics, holding the bar top so as not to fall off his stool. Breathless, he clapped a hand on my neck, and using me for leverage, thrust himself, half-stooped, laughing wildly, in a crooked line toward the coat rack. He slipped into his down coat—a gift from his fiancée, to keep him cozy abroad—and, pushing his weight against the door, stumbled into the night.

The younger brother did not come at the sound of the bell. I looked for him in the doorway, where the metal cart was positioned askew, as if shoved, or fallen upon. The floor was littered with glass, with tiny flecks of garnish strewn atop the shards. On the shelf sat no stereo, only speakers. On the floor, among green herbs and glass, was a black plastic dial. Off the edge of the shelf hung a black electrical cord, flaccid and detached, its prong dangling an inch or two above the cart.

I sat alone at the bar. The room was eerie in silence.

I heard sounds of distant chatter from the dining room, strangers eating meals, friends and families breaking bread and telling stories. I was drunk, of that I was certain, and my inebriation may have played a part in my apprehension—the invisible crowd, the phantom scents of caraway rolls and dill cream gravies, the chill in the air—and I felt, with no intellectual merit, a ghostly presence, the hairs on my arms standing on end as they had in the church earlier that night, when a beautiful blonde violinist played the crescendo in Vivaldi's "Winter" concerto.

The lights inside prevented me from seeing out the window on the wall opposite the pass, but I felt certain my friend was there, watching me, laughing or thumbing his nose, like when he won a hand in a card game, or the night Emily Abruzzo, the first girl we loved, chose *him* at the middle school dance. I waited for the younger brother to traipse through the kitchen doorway, brisket and dumplings in hand, a bounce in his step and a song in his heart. But he failed to return. I placed a 500-koruny note on the bar, grabbed my coat off the rack, and left.

It was snowing outside, fat clumps moist as spit wads. I walked a few blocks and found my friend in front of the Astronomical Clock, his face pink from the cold. He was gazing up at the clock with a childlike opulence, his shoulders quivering with aftershocks of laughter. I asked him what I had missed in the bar. He wiped his eyes with the tip of his scarf, and said, "You had to have *been* there," and left it at that. I rolled a snowball from the slush at my feet and threw it at his back. Shivering, I followed him out of the square.

We drifted along cold streets, slipping on icy cobblestones. We took a detour through Wenceslas Square, where the food vendors pitched their tents. My friend, ordering a smažený sýr, said, "I'm too damn hungry to be vegan tonight!" and between us we ate half a dozen fried cheese sandwiches in the cold square, huddled beside the vendors' wood fire grills. In the center of the square an area was roped off, and workers were preparing fireworks for the following day's New Year's Eve celebration. My friend and I walked to the top of the square, sat on the courthouse steps, and watched the men work, and the snow fall, and the smoke from the wood fires rise into whiteness. I asked one more time what I missed in the barroom.

"Use your imagination," he said, to which I replied, "Oh go to hell."

We stayed awake in our room playing war with a deck of airline cards, and telling stories, until we could keep our eyes open no longer. In the morning, we boarded separate flights to separate cities. I saw my friend at his wedding, and we swore an oath to return to Prague one day. But a few years into his marriage, while driving home from his office in Long Beach, a city bus T-boned his sedan. My friend died on impact. His wife—she told me at the funeral—was irritated with him that evening; he missed dinner, and she'd assumed he'd been working late again without calling. They were saving up to buy a house; he was in line for a promotion. She ate by herself, bitterly, and put their newborn son, Daniel, to bed. It was 8 p.m. when an officer rang the doorbell.

My friend took to his grave, among other things, the story of what happened that night in the pub. I'd asked him countless times to tell me, but all he'd say was, "Oh brother, one day."

[Lynne: Wrong Turn]

You're making me anxious. The last thing I need in life is to be more anxious.

SLOW FOOD

My father farts at the dinner table.

His mother, in her golden years, was given carte blanche to pass gas.

Her excuse? Partial colectomy.

When my father—a relatively healthy man—lets fly, he says, "Whoops."

I say, "Foul," and take away his plate.

I say, "Thirty seconds in the box."

My mother applauds, while my father sulks, appealing to the dog for recognition.

The man is a black hole. Potatoes, green beans, pork—heaping spoonfuls cross an event horizon at his lips and disappear, swallowed whole.

His plate is clean in sixty seconds.

He leans back, tilts in his chair, patting his stomach proudly. Then he farts again and leaves the table.

I've heard men speak of the winds of war, others of the winds of change.

What kinds of winds are his?

VISITING WRITER

When she narrowly avoided falling off the curb at the train station with a balletesque repositioning of her luggage and feet, I asked her how she'd come to achieve such balance.

She said, "Years of psychotherapy."

HABIT

In the summer of 1986, my father sold his shotgun. Earlier that year, in the dead of winter, he encountered a fox in our woods. He was circling a cluster of red osier dogwoods, scanning the entwined branches for grouse, when he spotted the fox crouched at the lip of a frozen pond, pawing at cracks in the ice. My father's approach had been hushed by an inch of freshly fallen snow, the fox's ears obscured behind a tent of dead, slanted cattails. My father, compelled by instinct, leveled his Remington. But the shot was in haste, at too close a range, and although the fox had magnificent fur—a fiery clementine—the buckshot tore its skin apart. The ruined pelt earned a pittance at our local bait and tackle (the shotgun later sold for twenty times as much). My father, consumed less by the pitiful trade than the ease with which the killing instinct overtook him, shied away from the woods until spring. It was a waste, he said, the whole damn thing, and he vowed never to kill an animal again. He still eats them.

[Woman, Sighing, Exiting a Hat Shop in Cambridge, Massachusetts]

I have a gigantic *head.*

FORGETTING

Branch had a dream about the dog. In the dream, the dog nearly died in a shoebox, where Branch stowed it when he left for Norway, a place he'd never been in real life. Returning from the snowy, far north, he opened the box, removing the dog: shriveled, forgotten, as thin as a pencil—but alive.

His wife tells him: "Now that we're in Alabama, you can visit the town where you left that dog of yours to die." In her defense, Branch had mentioned nursing homes, for her father—who'd just had a stroke. She'd been upset at Branch already, before the stroke, for taking a job so far from the Catskills, the only home she'd ever known. The move was hard on her. She missed her parents. She missed good pizza—and mountains. She even missed winter.

And it was true, Branch *had* abandoned a dog, years before he met his wife, when he was living in Iowa and in love with another woman. With the dog in tow, he'd driven overnight, in the dead of winter, through a storm that turned from snow to rain the farther south he traveled, on his way to the only no-kill shelter he could find, the owner having promised, over the phone, to care ad infinitum for the dog, who'd gone violent with age.

One month after he abandoned the dog, Branch found an article online about the shelter's owner: she was shooting dogs in her barn, burying them in unmarked graves. Branch never called to learn the fate of his dog. He knew in his heart the dog was dead.

Now, in another January, in another state, his wife tells him her father will need months of inpatient rehab. He's forgotten the names for things, what the doctors call aphasia. He calls the telephone *frog*, the toothbrush *moon*. It's the beginning of a long, convoluted road, not the sort of thing a man like Branch could foresee in the clouds while kneeling on the Hudson River shoreline, on a white winter day, asking for his lover's hand in marriage. But it is, as they say, *what it is*, and tonight, while his wife takes a bath—soaking in Epsom salts, sulking alone—Branch paces on the back porch with his nightly cigar, observing the stars.

As Cassiopeia burns too low in the sky, it dawns on him: this will be the first winter in his life he won't see snow. He tries to remember the first time he saw it, and what it felt like, as a boy, to watch the sky fall apart. But he can't recall. The grass in the yard is too green, the weather too warm. It's akin to aphasia, he thinks, winter forgetting its snow.

Branch puffs on his cigar, and tries to recall a Japanese word for snow. He took a Buddhism class in college, long ago, but all he knows is they had *lots* of words for snow, too many to recollect. A man must forget things in order to live, must strip things away to keep moving. And besides, he thinks, removing his coat, what use is a word like that when it only ever rains in Dixie?

RISE

My friend Erik taught me how to make challah bread.

"There are different methods," he said. "You'll learn to make your own adjustments."

Our *boule* was plump and taut, the size and shape of a starving child's belly.

"Before we braid it," said Erik, "tell me how we got here."

First we ran the tap until the water was warm; we measured one-and-a-half cups into a bowl; we added a quarter cup honey, a tablespoon yeast; we whisked; we added two cups high-gluten flour, whisking until the mass had a glue-like consistency; we covered the bowl with a damp kitchen towel, letting it rest in a warm oven for one hour.

"The pilot light will warm the glue?"

"The glue," Erik corrected, "is called a *sponge*."

When the sponge doubles in size, remove the bowl from the oven; the yeast should be well active, the sponge bubbling and popping like a mud spa and smelling faintly of beer; drizzle a third cup canola oil over the sponge; sprinkle a tablespoon kosher salt over the oil; using a spatula, fold the oil and salt into the sponge, a dozen or so gentle strokes; mix in a quarter cup powdered milk and two eggs; add three cups flour and fold the mixture until all the flour is incorporated; when a soft dough forms, plop the dough on the counter, dust with flour, and knead; work the dough until it's smooth and elastic—like an earlobe—adding flour as needed; tear off a piece of the dough, stretch it between your fingertips, and hold it to the light; if it resembles the wing of a bat, the dough is ready to rise.

"And if it doesn't resemble the wing of a bat?"

"Keep kneading."

SAUDADE

i.   In one dream, I do not recognize my sister when I pass her on the street.

ii. I wake at 3 a.m. as the dog leaps out of bed: a dash to the kitchen, a violent lapping at his water dish—as if he'd traveled far in his dreams, thousands of miles, an Odyssean journey, and he'd just then, at that very moment, at long last, reached home. This happens nightly.

iii. My mother told me that when her father got drunk, he'd strip naked and sleep in the yard. When my sister got high, she'd sit in our parents' basement, eating almonds and watching *Blind Date*.

iv. My challah bread doughs [seven braids] were too wet: the crusts kept burning before the insides cooked through. You'd think I'd have learned over time. If not that, something.

v.   Paul renamed the dog he got from the shelter. "*Boner*," he said, "had been through enough."

vi. I told Jordan I had a dream my daughter was missing. Jordan said he'd also had a dream; in his dream he was trying to feed his infant son a three-foot-wide hamburger bun.

vii. My sister, before she died, had a conspiracy theory about the band *NSYNC. They were robots, she claimed, their names were the clue: Timberlake had a smooth, pure timbre; Joey Fatone was the "fat one"; Lance Bass sang "bass." I asked her what about JC Chasez and Chris Kirkpatrick. "Oh, they were real," she said. "But they were in on it."

[The Rhetorician's Desire]

I've developed a decision matrix to help quantify my feelings.

WOMEN

Anna from Poland taught him not to watch the mugs while serving: stare at the lip and your hands will tremble.

Janelle taught him how to cold-brew.

Heidi taught him how to clean a sink with lemon peels.

Marie from Paris taught him it's OK in a pinch to use a percolator.

Amy taught him how to fall in love (with Ethiopian Yirgacheffe).

Kate taught him that no matter how much time and effort you invest in something, someone will prefer McDonald's.

Cynthia taught him how to use an em dash.

Cassie taught him how to order from the secret menu.

His mother taught him how to salve a wound with garlic cloves.

In a booth inside a Denny's restaurant, in Upstate New York, when he was sixteen years old, his first girlfriend taught him how to "milk the cow" with half-and-half containers.

And it was Chingbee, twenty years later, flying home to Manila in the midst of a civil war, who taught him that the true price of passion is self-annihilation.

He'd tell you this much: drink it fast or learn to love it lukewarm—hot or cold, it all grows tepid over time.

THE MOTHER CUP

In class today, the teacher was asked about his mug. The mug was a gift from his mother, a Christmas present long ago. The mug was brown, with a big green handle. It was a good mug, a heavy mug, a mug made of clay. His students enjoyed the fact that he drank out of the same mug every day; no matter what uncertainties they faced in their outside lives, there sat the teacher, there the mug, three times a week, like clockwork.

When asked about the mug's significance, the teacher replied: "It holds my tea." The student—a young woman, from Israel—said, "I mean the *history* of the mug. Where it came from." Sitting at his desk in a circle of twenty students, in a small room in a large university, the overhead lights off and the windows open, the teacher took a slow, calculated sip of lapsang souchong (his students recognized that brew, its smoky aroma) and thought about his mother.

As a boy, for Christmas, he'd given his mother a cookie jar shaped like a penguin. It was the first gift he ever bought with his own money (five one-dollar bills, each a lost tooth). His mother filled the jar with homemade macaroons, reserved a place for it atop the microwave. She loved the jar, and told him often—and at night he'd climb down the stairs in the dark of the house to stare at the jar by the glow of the microwave's clock, with the scent of coconut in the air, and he'd be flush with a feeling he could not articulate until much later in life. A reverent feeling, a feeling of *home*.

In mid-January, he broke the jar playing sock hockey on the kitchen's smooth tile floor (his father's putter for a stick, a tuna can puck) when he slid sideways into the microwave cart, an accidental hip-check that set the penguin wobbling, like a poorly spun coin, until it toppled, falling between his outstretched arms and crashing headlong at his feet. The penguin broke in such a way that the fragments of its skull were covered over by its buttocks, which landed, intact, upside down.

Unaccustomed to the fault of misplaced value, the boy ached with incipient sadness as he stared down at the ruins. His father, noting the penguin's headless rump, improvised a joke about an ostrich, a mood his mother reinforced, telling a story about a special penguin who dug holes in, and peered under, the surface of ice rinks, hungry for krill. The boy was inconsolable.

What to tell a twenty-year-old? As the teacher, he could quote the masters, he could ring the old bells, he could quiet the room with cadence and pomp. But that would not do. She, his student, had asked for *history*, not song—the mug, the mother, the taut throat of rising action, the pollinated hush of denouement. Still, he could *narrate* the damned thing in his sleep, removed from the pain of experience—the years, the loss, the dead—detached and articulate, dispassionate, *true*.

With this in mind, the teacher took a long, deep breath, savoring the wood fire scent of the tea, then he set the mug on his desk, balled his fist, scanned the room until he met each pair of eyes in the circle, and using his knuckles he pushed, slowly, the mug across the desk's surface, inching it closer and closer to the ledge, careful not to spill its contents, the pace of his movements dictated by the weight of the mug's resistance, while his students, rapt, leaned in, their soft bodies bending toward the center of the ring of desks, their eyes on the mug, a few among them lifting a hand as if to stop him.

[Saving Grace]

At the grocery store, in the checkout line, an elderly woman points at his slippers, saying, "Swamp donkeys."

"Pardon me?"

"Swamps donkeys," she repeats. "Alces alces. *Two moose."*

It's 2 p.m. on a Tuesday. He contemplates his footwear. Then to the woman, who he receives with a kindness, as if she were his mother, he says, "Some days moose *are all I can* mustard.*"*

UNA VIDA MEJOR

I'm sitting in a plastic chair at a fold-out table in my sister's kitchen, eating pizza out of the box. It's a hot and humid summer day in Richmond, and the apartment lacks an air conditioner. My sister keeps the windows shut, the curtains drawn. She tosses me a mandarin Jarritos soda from a six-pack on the counter, sliding a rusty bottle opener across the tabletop. The Jarritos bottle is a twist cap. I use the opener to be polite.

"Baby want sauce?" she asks. "For the crust."

I tell her, "Ranch."

She tilts her chair back, opens a compact fridge, squirts a little dressing on a napkin. The dressing is runny, off-color. I slide the bottle opener to my sister, and I fold the napkin over when she isn't looking.

When we're done eating, my sister balances the pizza box on a stack of take-out containers piled high atop the garbage can. She has a black heart tattooed on her chest, the first she ever got, back in high school. When she met Zeb, years later, she had the heart engulfed in blue flames, the tips of which are visible at her neckline as she leans forward to put the leftover slices in the fridge.

"You maybe wanna wrap those first?"

Ignoring me, she grabs a pack of Rolos from the butter

compartment. She peels the golden foil, pops a candy in her mouth. She tosses one in my direction but it lands on the floor behind me.

"Hey," she says, slamming the fridge. "*¡Hoy es mi cumpleaños!* Pobrecito's teaching me."

I tell her, "Your birthday is in March."

"Not if it gets me better tips."

She shrugs me off while I think of a joke. She misinterprets my silence.

"Don't worry," she says, her mouth full of caramel. "I've lied about worse."

Later, she tells me people treat Pobrecito like a dog because he's got no record, and she gets treated like a dog because she *has* a record. Pobrecito lived in a garage when they met. She lived in a women's safe house. She tells me it's like *Lady and the Tramp*, only there's no lady.

"Do you remember," I say, changing the subject, "the time Buster got his head stuck in the milk jug?"

"Who's Buster?"

Buster was our family beagle. We found him at an animal shelter. Pobrecito and my sister found one another on the midnight shift. She says he'd hang around the kitchen after clocking out until she finished her side work, just to walk her home safely. His real name is Pablo—like Neruda. But my sister gets mixed up between Neruda and Jorge Luis Borges. I tell her Borges wrote those stories about labyrinths and libraries, tigers and wars. I tell her Neruda wrote love poems, he wrote "Tonight I Can Write (the Saddest Lines)" and I remind her she owned the *Il Postino* soundtrack on cassette, and that we'd ride to school together in her VW Jetta taking turns doing our worst impressions of Andy Garcia, who read for the soundtrack. She denies owning the cassette tape, but she *knows* who Borges is. Neruda was a blind historian.

"You're right," I tell her, tapping the side of my head. "I get confused sometimes."

My sister gets up from the table, opens a drawer, retrieves a pack of Newports.

"*Hermano*," she says, slapping the pack on her palm. "Join the club."

I wash my hands in the bathroom but the towel smells unclean. I dry my hands on my jeans, below the knees so my sister won't notice. The bathroom opens into the kitchen.

"Close the door," she says. "Gross."

"I only washed my hands."

"*Close* it."

The knob slips from my fingers and the door bangs shut. On the night Zeb died, my sister tested positive for gunshot residue. In her report to the police she claimed she had been trying to pull the gun away from Zeb's head when he pulled the trigger. Zeb spent forty-eight hours on life support and my sister twice that long in jail until a forensic investigation failed to discredit her story. Zeb's death was ruled a suicide and my sister was released in time for the funeral. I saw her there, but kept my distance, and when Zeb was in the ground, she disappeared. Four years later she calls me out of the blue and says, "You hungry?"

She's sitting at the table, counting playing cards.

"Deck's short," she says, looking left, and right. "I need a pen."

An IHOP mug filled with pens and plastic cutlery sits on a ledge above the sink.

"Red," she tells me.

There's no red pen. Reluctantly, she uses blue to write the number 9 in the corner of a joker card, and draws a heart around it. I sit across from her and watch while she draws three more 9s, and three more hearts, until the card is complete. She draws a big blue heart around the joker in the middle, then shuffles.

I knock every other hand and this irritates her. She accuses me of cheating.

"Sorry," I say. "College education."

The next time I knock, she undercuts me, gaining twenty-five points plus three from my hand.

"Prison education," she says.

We continue to play, and after a while I'm winning big. I expect her to get bored, like when we were kids, or to come down with one of her headaches, but she's into the game, popping Rolos, tallying our scores on a legal pad. I'm the one who's getting tired. It's dark in her apartment, and humid, and it smells like wet carpet, and each time the conversation lags, I feel the car keys in my pocket digging sharply into my leg.

Eventually I tell her, "I'm tired of keeping score."

She turns the pad over, says, "We'll keep it in our heads."

We deal in silence for twenty more minutes, and I tell her, "I'm pretty sure you won."

I accept a soda for the road, but I refuse to let her pay for the pizza.

"I'm *earning* now," she says.

"It's on me," I say.

"Hey hey," she says, clapping loudly. "My younger brother, ladies and gentleman."

She walks me to the door, which is double-deadbolted, security-chained, and blocked by a metal chair she'd lodged under the handle when I first entered. The light in the hallway is clean and bright, and it takes a moment for my eyes to adjust.

"Let's not hug," she says.

She shuts the door, then reopens it an inch with the security chain in place. I wait while she lights a cigarette, crossing my arms in a display of brotherly disapproval.

"*Hermana*," I say, cocking my head. "Tell me, this guy—is he good to you?"

My sister wedges her face in the crack of the door and exhales.

"He's illegal," she says, as I step away from the smoke. "He's got a wife and kids in Juárez. He sends them money, and letters. He lets me read the letters out loud, for practice."

I hear movement in the hallway behind me, the scuff of footsteps, the shuffling of keys.

I ask her, "Do they write him letters back?"

"*No sé*," she says, shutting the door.

Two dead bolts and a chair.

Acknowledgments

Heartfelt thanks to the editors of the following journals, where many of these stories first appeared:

Barzakh, Blue Earth Review, BULL, Chautauqua, The Chattahoochee Review, CutBank, Fiction International, Hobart, Inch, J Journal, Lalitamba, Mid-American Review, The Pinch, Storm Cellar, StoryGLOSSIA, Tammy, Thin Air Magazine, West Texas Literary Review

The italicized text on p. 53 of "Semiotic Love" is from *A Dictionary of Narratology*, by Gerald Prince (U of Nebraska, 2003). The italicized text on p. 16 of "Deep Water" is from *Moon in a Dewdrop: Writings of Zen Master Dogen*, edited by Kazuaki Tanahashi (North Point, 1995).

Special thanks to the team at Awst—Wendy, Tatiana, David, LK, and Phoebe—who helped shape this book and bring it into the world. Friends and family, of now and then, who have been there with me over the years or who have made lasting impacts appear, in distorted forms, within these stories, as a form of endearment. Nearly all of the stories in this collection began in workshop, and

I'd be remiss not to say thank you to all the readers who shared time with me in classrooms, and to my teachers, whose advice on writing is still, to this day, a source of inspiration, a light within that I rely on when the road gets dark: Paul Cody, Peter Cummings, Inman Majors, David Zimmerman, Steve Pett, Heather Derr-Smith, Lydia Davis—and the best mentors on this, or any, planet: Langdon Brown, Lynne Tillman, and Ed Schwarzschild.

About the Author

Brian Phillip Whalen's work can be found in the *Flash Nonfiction Food* anthology, *The Southern Review, Creative Nonfiction, Copper Nickel,* and elsewhere. Brian holds a PhD from the State University of New York at Albany and is the recipient of a Vermont Studio Center residency. He lives with his wife and daughter in Tuscaloosa where he teaches creative and first-year writing at The University of Alabama. This is his first book.

Website: www.brianphillipwhalen.com